Stone

Writing and art b

MW01064268

Editor's Note

Hello! I am beyond excited to introduce myself as the new editor of *Stone Soup!* I have been a fan of the magazine since I read it as a child, and I will never forget the feeling of wonder it gave me to discover that kids like me could be published authors. For many years, I worked as a children's book editor at a major publisher, so it has been a fun challenge for me to turn my attention to work by children. I am so impressed with your submissions!

This month, as befits the cooling weather, several of our pieces explore the longing for comfort—the historical story about a Jewish girl who searches for hope after being separated from her family by the Nazis; the widow who eases the pain of the loss of her husband through the creative process of embroidery; the orphan girl bringing what cheer she can to her aunt and uncle amidst the war in Ukraine; a poem called "Home."

Change is another theme authors explore this November. There's a story about how animals deal with the extreme weather they suffer due to climate change. There are poems about changing seasons, changing friendship, a changing world. What changes have you experienced, and what comforts you through them?

D Landolf

Thank You to Our Donors!

Production and publication of this issue is made possible by our Jane Austen donors ($1,000 and above):

The Allen & Eve Foundation, Sandy & Tom Allen, Anonymous (4), James Evarts, Amanda Fox, Brian Harlan, Gerry Mandel, Brion Sprinsock & Kristine Albrecht, and Sally & Clem Wood.

Cover:
Peace (Oil)
Ivory Vanover, 12
Texas

Executive Director
Emma Wood

Editor
Diane Landolf

Operations
Sophia Opitz

Production Coordinator
Carmela Furio

Typesetter
Jeff Piekarz

Communications
Tayleigh Greene

Blog Editor
Caleb Berg

Refugee Project
Laura Moran

Director Emeritus
William Rubel

Stone Soup (ISSN 0094 579X) is published bimonthly, six times per year. Copyright © 2023 by the Children's Art Foundation–Stone Soup Inc., a 501(c)(3) nonprofit organization located in Santa Cruz, California. All rights reserved.

Thirty-five percent of our subscription price is tax-deductible. Consider further supporting *Stone Soup*—visit stonesoup.com/donate.

To request the braille edition of *Stone Soup* from the National Library of Congress, call +1 800-424-8567. To request access to the audio edition via the National Federation of the Blind's NFB-NEWSLINE®, call +1 866-504-7300, or visit Nfbnewsline.org.

StoneSoup
Contents

Scan this QR code to access educational material for this painting.

Peekaboo My Pumpkin (Oil pastel)
Leticia Cheng, 10
California

Halloween Guilt

When neighbors leave Halloween candy unattended, how much is right to take?

By Yanling Lin, 12
Virginia

Every year on Halloween night, I spot something bewildering. I spot something that makes me audibly gasp, guffaw, or simply gawk. This year was no exception. The moment took place long into the night, catching me more off guard than usual.

Rewinding back to earlier during Halloween evening, I sat by the window watching the sun set. I had scarfed down dinner and pulled on my costume, only to wait for my mom to finish as well.

"The candy will still be there in fifteen minutes," my mom told me. That was easy for her to say. She was only a bystander in the game of gathering sweet treats from neighbors. I was a player. After enough pleas and other people going outside, we finally joined the parade. The golden glow of the sun waving "goodnight" kept my breathing even. In my mind, I had all night to collect sweets from around the neighborhood. I sauntered along the sidewalk, letting the giddy five- and six-year-olds sprint past, knowing they had to be in bed by nine o'clock.

As darkness descended, I became those giddy kids running from door to door. The night was growing, and so was my desire for candy. I passed numerous empty houses as I traipsed down the unlit sidewalks. With each step I heard my boots scratching against the ground, creating a rhythmic *thump-thump*. The bag handles sank into my flesh, slowing me down. That didn't stop me from going on. I half-skipped between doorsteps, my "Trick or treat!" bouncing as I spoke it. I powered through the night because within those dark alleys were the treasure troves of Halloween.

Many of these dark houses were accompanied by bowls of candy. Attached to these bowls were signs saying "Please Take 1" (or "2," if I was lucky). These directions posed a moral dilemma. As I dug through the bowls, I wondered, *Do I follow my own goals, or obediently do as told?*

The devil on my right shoulder would respond, "Take as much as you want. Everyone else probably does that too. Besides, the homeowner won't know."

The angel on the left argued, "Just because everyone else does it doesn't mean you should. The homeowner just wants everyone to get the same amount of candy!"

Perhaps I was influenced by the demonic costumes I had passed that night, but the devil got its way. These voices took me back to every time I was on the playground, thinking about sitting on top of the monkey bars or standing on the swings. Those same voices bantered, the devil winning. On the playground, the hawk eyes of my teacher had caused the dilemma. Getting caught was always a risk. Here, what risk did I have? There was no one to scold me for my actions, except for the angel, who was not surprised, just disappointed. Besides my mental angel, though, I could also envision the disappointed faces of potential parents who might have witnessed those crimes. I did not want to hear the bitterness laced into their scolding voices.

I kept pondering the situation as I dug through the bowl like a racoon, looking *for* York Peppermint Patties and looking *past* Twizzlers and lollipops. I could taste my mint-chocolate reward as the cubes of chocolate ran around my foraging hands. In my mind, I had to push the dirt away to find the diamonds. When leaving the scene of the crime, the angel pounded on the door of my mind, refusing to be shut away; after all, it was not wrong. As I contemplated, though, someone else's angel might not have even had a say.

I saw a young boy skipping towards a house with an unmanned candy bowl which I had just left. *Will he do as told, or be self-serving like me?* I wondered. I gaped at what he did next, though. With full confidence, he grabbed the entire bowl and in mere moments poured all the candy into his bag and dashed off.

Immediately, I wondered if I should have done the same. Though the extra candy would be heavier, I could trade it with my brother to get what I treasured most. Now, rather than feeling slightly guilty for my actions, I wished I could have done what he did. I wished I'd had the nerve to do so without any mental quandaries. At the same time, I liked that my morals were strong enough to keep me from doing the same. By the time I left the cul-de-sac, I did not know whether I agreed with him or not, but I definitely could not have blamed him.

Seasons

By Gemma Crimmins, 10
North Carolina

Winter, winter, coming clear,

come outside, what do you hear?

Wind whistles through the trees,

a robin tweets, no more freeze.

Spring has come as small as a hum,

and too fast, summer is second to last,

summer, summer, fall's the last.

Who knew the year could pass so fast?

Winter, winter, coming fast,

the old year's in the past . . .

Veil over Valley (OPPO Find X2 Lite)
Savarna Yang, 13
New Zealand

Seasons

As the seasons change, the animals must face extreme weather conditions.

By Chris Yihan Ye, 11
China

There was once a spring so windy the fields were empty, the people were lifted off their feet, and the sky was dotted with flying leaves.

"My god," Mole exclaimed as he hopped frantically back into his hole. He wiped at his frizzled fur. "I almost got blown away!"

"What's wrong, Mole?" asked Worm, who had just poked his head out of the ground.

"The outside has become chaotic! Now here is a windy spring, so windy that I can't go out without almost getting blown away!" Mole exclaimed as he jumped up and down. "I shall never be able to go out again. We will certainly starve to death this spring."

"What about the food you saved last winter?" Worm asked quizzically. He had never worried about starving; for as long as he could remember, the soil all around him was abundant with food.

"We finished it all!" Mole sobbed. "Lord, what a season!"

"I'm sure that's fine. Groundhog will be willing to share," Worm offered.

"Groundhog? No, that's an insane idea!" Mole sulked. Mole and Groundhog had long been enemies, and besides, Mole hated Groundhog's food. "I shall go cry in a corner and wish that the Lord would bless me, but thank you for your kindness."

And with that, Mole blew his nose and dug a nice archway by the side of the tunnel to sit in and pray. Worm sighed. He thought Mole was being overdramatic and too proud and stubborn to ask for help. Worm continued his little journey through the soil.

There was once a summer so hot that the sun burned red and the ground was cracked and the trees melted into icky, yellow glue.

One day, Eagle's eggs fell from her nest into the icky, yellow glue. She flapped her wings maniacally and screeched: "Eep! In the name of my feathers, we have just survived a Spring of Wind! Now this! A boiling summer, so hot that the sun is now red, the ground has cracked, and the trees have melted!"

Just then, Snail was taking a nice trip on the scorching ground. She looked up at the yelping, fuming eagle, who stared down enviously at Snail.

"How are you able to walk on the scorching ground?" Eagle demanded. Snail blinked.

"I have a trail of slime on me," Snail squeaked. "What about you? What is wrong?"

"My eggs have fallen into the icky glue the trees have melted into! And now I have no place to rest, as all the trees have melted, and the ground is too hot," Eagle wailed.

"You could go stand on a house!" Snail offered.

"Oh, no. The houses are made out of bricks!" Eagle screeched. "Oh, no. The sun's scorching temperature against that? What a joke!"

"Ah, but you could use some of my slime!" Snail offered again.

"Your slime?" Eagle stopped wailing for a while and considered the notion, scrunching up her beak in disgust. "I won't be able to touch the ground. No, thank you."

And so Eagle continued being pessimistic and flew away in despair to find a friend to share this complaint with. Snail shook her head and continued pushing herself forward.

There was once a fall so cool that the trees bent down and the polar bears shivered, and the people wore three jackets each time they went out.

"What season is it?" Orca asked Tuna Fish, shivering.

"It's fall!" Tuna Fish replied in the same shaky voice. "Why, I'm going to die from the cold! Fish don't feel cold, do they?"

"I suppose not," Orca shivered back. "But I am a mammal, and so I do."

"If I may ask, do you migrate?" Tuna Fish asked as it started to swim in mini-circles to get warmed up.

"Yes!" Orca wailed. "First a Spring of the Wind, a Summer of the Red Sun, and now a Fall of Coolness? The cold will definitely prevent us from migrating without dying."

"You've got a big brain," Tuna Fish pointed out. "You've got to be able to think of something."

Now Orca started to swim in circles in deep pondering. "You are right. I am going to call upon my pod for a meeting. We must find a way to thrive using the deep waters as a habitat this season."

"But won't the cold water here"—Tuna Fish paused before continuing—"bring death upon you too?"

Orca stopped swimming and let out an exasperated sob before continuing to swim at a rapid speed, so fast people would've thought he was insane.

"So be it!" the orca said shakily. "We all die one day. But at the moment, I'm very, very hungry."

And so Orca gobbled Tuna Fish up and went to his pod to declare the devastating conclusions.

There was once a winter so cold that the trees downright froze and all the animals got frostbite, and the snow froze blue.

House Dog barked and barked and nibbled hopelessly on the door, feeling desperate after almost an entire year of being stuck indoors, but it would not budge. He sighed and flopped onto a nearby sofa, exhausted.

"I told you not to try and open the door!" purred House Cat. "Now you're tired."

"Well, enlighten me! How will we get outside of the house, then?" House Dog cried out as he rolled over off the couch.

"Here is a freezing winter, one so cold there are only frozen trees, animals with frostbite, and blue snow. Our house has been covered with too much ice for us to open the door and go outside," said House Cat.

"What?" House Dog asked, shocked. He sat up and started to sulk. "I shall never get my daily walk again! A Spring of the Wind, a Summer of the Red Sun, a Fall of the Bending Trees, and now a Winter of the Blue Snow? Why, life can be cruel!"

"I live perfectly fine without a walk," House Cat said proudly. "And you will too."

"You're a cat!" House Dog yelped again, devastated. "Easy for you to say! I require walks and sunlight and warmth, but now all those are forever gone for the season."

"Well, why don't we just enjoy the fact we have our home and wait for the next spring?" House Cat suggested. "I'm sure we have enough things at home to fill our winter."

And so the two sat on the couch with their tails dangling off the couch as they stared out the window and watched the blue snow fall gently to the ground.

Quite Adorable (Graphite pencil)
Tutu Lin, 13
Texas

Inna's Fast-Flowing Stream

Inna seeks comfort in the midst of war in Ukraine.

By Ayla Fardin, 10
California

I woke at 6 a.m., a very chilly time to be awake. I hate waking at this hour, but most of the time I can't help it. It is so chilly that it is uncomfortable to stay asleep, but I would rather hide under the covers and my pillow than have to suffer through sirens and shouting.

I was awake now, though, and I couldn't do anything about it. I pushed myself up out of bed and staggered sleepily to the kitchen. I live in an apartment probably the size of someone's living room, if not smaller.

I went into our tiny kitchen. The kitchen is my favorite room in the apartment, because it is the warmest, and because I'm always soothed by the smells of Auntie's special teas that she only lets me and my uncle drink on our birthdays. (They leave the most beautiful scents in the house.)

I was surprised to see my uncle and aunt already up, sitting at the kitchen table. In front of them, they had a pile of newspapers, our radio, and the mini-TV we owned turned on atop the cramped kitchen counter—basically everything you could receive news from in our apartment. And the most questionable, concerning part about it was that they had their whole pile of savings in front of them. This made me frightened.

They glanced up at me. Their eyes had big circles under them. Their faces were red, and it looked like they had been crying. This all shocked me. I had a painful stomachache slowly coming on. I experience these when I feel stressed, sad, or basically any emotion conjured up that is upsetting. These stomachaches usually feel like something is punching and wrenching into my stomach slowly but surely.

"Good morning, sweetie pie." Auntie yawned.

"Morning," I replied sheepishly.

I meant to say it in a kind tone, but it came out wrong. (I often have trouble with this.)

I opened a cupboard and pulled out some oatmeal mix. I then put some water on the stove in a pan to boil. After a couple minutes of waiting, I poured the oatmeal in and put the lid on top. I had oatmeal every day for breakfast. My aunt and uncle always had a rushed breakfast, so they just had coffee and sometimes split a piece of toast. This morning, however, they didn't have one single piece of food on the table—not even coffee!

As I waited for my oatmeal to cook, I made myself a small cup of Moroccan mint tea. (I had this every morning with my oatmeal.) I put only one sugar cube in it. I used to put two, but now, since Auntie and Uncle aren't working, we have to cut back on things that are not necessary. These cubes were the last of the ones we had bought last week.

After I finished making my tea, I scooped the oatmeal out of the pot and set it in a bowl. I carried my breakfast to the table and took the last vacant seat.

I started to eat when my ear caught something. I looked up after hearing the key word that had basically taken over my life: war. I glanced at the TV. My heart fell at what I saw. I dropped my spoon and ran to my room. As I ran, I caught a glance of Auntie and Uncle staring at each other, their faces etched with worry.

I picked up my favorite stuffy, Possy—the only thing I had left that made me feel comforted and strong. I've always loved how Possy's ears are yellow and how her tail is blue. It reminds me of home. Every Christmas, no matter how old I was, Mom would always get me a stuffed animal with our home—Ukraine's—colors on them. Possy was the last one she got me and it still smelled like her. Unlike every other time, though, this time when I was curled up with Possy, petting and clutching her to my chest, I felt a ping of sadness instead of comfort. Tears took over my face.

Auntie stood in my doorway. There grew a silence, making the air in the room thick and hard. She came up to me and sat down on my bed. She pulled me into her and stroked my hair. Then, Uncle walked into the doorway, and after a little while, he came and curled up on the other side of me. I felt better but not recovered.

We did this a lot. I have had a lot of emotional hours ever since I moved in. Luckily, Auntie and Uncle understand, and don't seem to ever grow tired of comforting me.

We all stayed huddled as a pack until I suddenly pulled away.

"What are you guys doing? I need to know," I inquired. I meant it in a firm way, but it came out very shaky.

Uncle sighed and glanced at Auntie. Auntie sighed too, and then took a deep breath.

"We are looking for ways to leave the country."

I swallowed. I knew that this war was not safe, but I had never imagined leaving the place where I had grown up. The place where I had made all my great memories. The place where my life was planted. This was the worst news I could get at the worst time of my life.

"We know that this news is hard for you, so we're going to give you your space for a little while. But, of course, if you need us, we're always here," Uncle finished.

My aunt nodded. They then both kissed me on the forehead and lifted themselves off the bed.

After they left, I just sat on my bed. I looked at my watch. The time was 7:45 a.m. I clutched Possy with my sweating, trembling hands. I felt my eyelids grow heavy.

I felt weird and slightly lightheaded when I awoke. I hadn't realized that I was so tired. I glanced at my watch: 9:23! I couldn't believe that I had slept that much. I guess I had a lot going on in my mind and that was what was tiring me out. Plus, it's very hard to sleep with all these noises of war.

I scooched to the other side of my twin bed to get my book. Books were the only thing that were getting me through all this. I loved them. As I scooched, I got a big jolt when something moved under my covers! I pulled up the sheet and inspected underneath. There, my aunt and uncle's dog, Fern, was snoring softly, snuggled up with her chew toy. I smiled. I had loved Fern ever since I moved in, and I found her to be the most patient and understanding creature out of all of us. To be frank, any dog or animal is. They do not want anything but love, and they only want to give you love and joy. In my opinion, they are better than humans in those terms.

I kept scooching slowly until I reached my bedside table. There, as I reached for my book, I froze. As I looked at the table, there stood a picture of my family. My *whole* family. My *mom*, my *dad*, my aunt and my uncle. After COVID-19, my aunt and uncle were the only family I had left.

I was about to burst into tears when I caught my aunt sitting at the edge of my bed watching me. I couldn't believe I hadn't noticed. I wiped away the small wet drops that had formed in my eyes. I quickly crawled across my bed to my aunt. She pulled me close. We sat like that for a while. Then, she pulled me up so I was facing her.

"I know this may be too quick, but we are going to go down to the train station to see if we can get a ride out soon."

I shook. This was all too much. I had too many things going on.

I didn't even think about it, but I nodded. She smiled slightly. I lifted myself off the bed, and so did she.

"I guess I should get dressed," I sighed.

Auntie nodded and tiptoed to the door. I slid under my sheets and retrieved Fern. I loved that dog. I gently placed him down on the carpet (he continued to snore) and started making my bed. After that, I quickly pulled out a skirt and turtleneck (my everyday outfit). I then hopped out of my room and took a few steps to our shared bathroom. As I walked in, I almost fainted. My uncle was standing in front of the mirror half *naked*, with his towel wrapped around his waist. I have seen this every day since I moved in but still haven't digested it. The crazy thing about this is that my uncle always forgets that he's half naked.

"I'll be out of your way in just a moment," he greeted me. I tossed my hair aside so it wouldn't go in my mouth and nodded. He quickly finished combing his hair and trudged out of the bathroom—his hairy back jiggling as he went.

I quickly washed my face and hands. Then, I got out my favorite headband (we all have our own little basket in the bathroom) and put it in my hair.

As I did that, a thought occurred to me. I wondered what outside would be like. Not just because of the war but because I haven't been outside that much ever since I've moved in. I have been grieving. I couldn't believe that after all this, my aunt and uncle thought that I could go outside. *Did they even think it was safe?*

I had so many thoughts going on in my brain that I felt like I couldn't take any more. But of course, more just kept on coming. After I finished getting ready, I walked down the cramped hall to my aunt and uncle's bedroom. I played with my skirt a bit and then knocked.

"Come in!" Auntie said sweetly. I walked in and sat on the chair of my uncle's desk.

"I'm all set, I guess."

"All right." My auntie smiled. "I'll go check on your uncle."

As I waited, my eye caught something on Uncle's desk. A piece of paper—folded and refolded many times—was laying on the desk. I shifted my body so I could read it.

My heart stopped. My stomach grumbled. Everything ached. There, on the paper, were the details of all of our savings in my aunt's neat handwriting:

```
To Evacuate A Person:  36,500 Hryvnia Per Ticket
To Evacuate An Animal:  12,400 Hryvnia Per Ticket
Total Amount For Evacuation:  221,900 Hryvnia
How Much We Have: 100,000 Hryvnia
Amount Needed:  121,900 Hryvnia
```

I couldn't stop shaking.

As I heard their footsteps, I realized that it would be horrible if my aunt and uncle knew I had seen this, so I pushed in the desk chair, smoothed out the ruffled cushion on it, and sat on the bed—pretending to be interested in one of Auntie's embroideries.

Right as I was reminding myself not to look so shaken, they came back and Auntie extended her hand.

I held her hand as we all walked out the apartment door and into the hallway.

I kept holding her hand as we descended the stairwell.

When we reached the bottom, I hesitated. I took a step back. The last time I had walked through this door was the day I had found out that my parents were dead.

I felt a hand on my shoulder. I glanced up. My aunt was smiling down at me.

"It's okay, Inna," she said.

We all were like connected keychains—each of us had a different picture and shape, but we were linked together.

I was frozen. I looked down to see a drop of water on my skirt. This was like a heap of emotion and memories all being dumped on me at once.

I slowly took a step forward and then another. With each step, I could feel more droplets falling on my skirt.

My uncle came over and took my free hand. We all were like connected keychains—each of us had a different picture and shape, but we were linked together.

We stopped as we reached the door.

I held my breath.

My aunt bent down and whispered into my ear.

"Are you sure you can handle this?"

I thought about it before nodding. I actually paused. I wasn't sure. I knew that we weren't going to be able to evacuate, and I didn't really even trust that I could pull myself together. I was also scared of what might be outside that door. If it was anything like what I have been hearing from the apartment, I knew I might not be able to bear it.

"Inna!"

Auntie sounded rushed, though I could tell she wanted her voice to be gentle.

I snapped back to attention. Even though I wasn't sure at all, I nodded. I had to be there for my aunt and uncle.

I took a deep breath, and Uncle opened the door.

Now I was on the verge of a mental breakdown. This was impossible. Outside, in front of me, was the same regular city I have seen all my life. People were going to work and mothers were pushing their babies in strollers. Dog owners were walking their dogs. It was all normal. The only thing that was different was that everyone looked sad and somber. I looked up at my aunt and uncle and they looked sad too.

We started walking. As we walked, I slowly felt less shaken.

Then, out of nowhere, we heard sirens and screaming from afar. I trembled. My aunt held my hand tight.

"It's not close," she reassured me.

We kept walking until, finally, Uncle stopped.

"Here we are," he stated.

We were in front of a big, steep staircase. We started going down until we were at the last step. We walked to the ticket booth.

"Excuse me," Auntie called out to the teller—her voice polite but firm.

I had never heard her talk this way. I felt a nudge on my shoulder.

"While your auntie's talking, why don't we look around a bit? It might be fun," my uncle suggested.

I could tell he was ordering me to do this and not asking. I guessed that this was because he didn't want me to hear about how we maybe couldn't afford to leave.

I took his hand and we started walking.

I felt sad. The last time I had been in a train station was the day that I had found out that my parents had died. We kept walking around until my Uncle stopped.

"Why don't we play a hopping game?"

"That sounds fun," I managed to say.

We made up a game where you had to make it across all the green tiles in the station by only hopping once in each square tile. I let Uncle win. He seemed delighted. Unlike Auntie, Uncle was always competitive in games no matter who he was up against. (I liked this about him.)

We went back to where Auntie was. When we saw her, she looked stricken. She shook her head at Uncle.

My guess was that they had come here because they wanted to make sure that they had the correct information about how much it would cost to leave the country. It all made me very sad.

We walked back home in silence. Bad thoughts seemed to race each other in my brain. *Were we stuck in Ukraine? Were we stuck in war? Were we even safe?*

When I was six, my mom told me that my name means "fast-flowing stream" in Ukrainian. I've never understood how my name fits me except that I think it does describe the way my thoughts work. I always seem to have a stream of thoughts instead of one at a time.

When we got home, I went into my bedroom—where Fern was wagging his tail behind the door. I decided to read for the rest of the afternoon. Even though I usually hate naps, I have to admit that the one I took in the morning really helped my energy. My book was okay. It was about a girl who was my age—eleven—and who had just lost her best friend because a bunch of sassy girls had swallowed her up and turned her into a sassy girl like them. It was a little crazy. I didn't like the storyline at all—partly because it was so different and unimaginable from my life. I didn't have any friends now, though I used to have many before I moved. This book actually made me sadder, so I decided to go and try to play a card game with Uncle.

As I played Uno with my uncle, I started to feel better bit by bit. I realized that maybe the war could end, or maybe we could keep saving up and evacuate later. The more I thought about it, I was happy we weren't leaving Ukraine. The people who were attacking us should be leaving and not the people like us, whose homes were here. I felt better now.

I decided to go back to my book. As I went back into my bedroom, a wonderful idea occurred to me: what if I made my aunt and uncle a fun surprise to lighten their mood? Since they had been working so hard and were so worried, they definitely deserved that.

After a dinner of beef stew, I went to bed thinking about the things that I could do for my aunt and uncle. The perfect thought occurred to me! Tomorrow, I would go outside and get the ingredients (from my allowance) for an omelet. It was one of Auntie's favorite dishes, and Uncle loved cooking it. Perhaps it would brighten their mood! I hoped they would sleep in tomorrow . . .

The next morning at 6 a.m., a very chilly time to be awake, I did not try to hide under the covers and my pillow. I got out of bed, quietly dressed myself, stepped out into the empty hall, walked down the stairwell to the door to everything outside and, determined, went on my way. I would buy eggs and tomatoes this morning and, as I did, I hoped I could lighten some of the moods around me in the streets and hopefully back at our apartment too.

A Light to Hope By (Pastel)
Leticia Cheng, 10
California

Where I'm From

By Anthony Halkos, 9
Atlanta, Georgia

I am from the teddy bear that is gigantic
From old dishes from Greece
I am from the calm wind that blows by my house
And the swing that went away in the waves of our pool
I am from the huge pine tree in the backyard that litters the ground
I am from the old luggage bag that came from Greece
From Alex and Penny, Uncle Matthew and Auntie Denise
And from traveling and books, from the spanakopita at Thanksgiving
I am from Uncle George saying a prayer at family gatherings
From apple pie that makes the house smell like apples
From traveling to America from Greece, and
From the fallen leaves on the family, and
the family tree that came from Greece,
the family tree that came from my grandparents' house
I am from moments at my Uncle Jimmy's house
I am from the family tree that is 567 years old
I am from Greece.

*Scan this QR code to access educational
material for this poem.*

Home

By Bethel Daniel, 12
Virginia

After school, you go
Home.
You feel safe when you are
Home.
After a long day, you go
Home.
When you're tired, you want to go
Home.
When you are on the road, you want to go
Home.
When you're at school, you want to go
Home.
When you are crying, you want to go
Home.
When you are hurting, you want to go
Home.
You are at peace when you are
Home.

Floral Night (Pen and pastel)
Riya Kasture, 12
India

Elephants/Shrews

By Mary G. Lane, 11
Virginia

At the zoo, there are elephants
And then there are elephant shrews
People come to see the elephants
Children point and throw peanuts
Adults take pictures
Elephants are on TV
Ever seen a shrew on TV?
And yet, the shrew is still there, looking at you,
Afraid to snuggle up by an elephant's foot
Where it wants to be
People look at the shrew and at the elephants.
An elephant stomps:
End of shrew.
But
When the people go home and
Write in diaries about their trip
They write about the elephants
And lionsandtigersandbears
But they also write about the shrew.

Bluetooth Menagerie (iPhone SE)
Amity Doyle, 13
New York

Two Poems

By Eloise (Ellie) Barnett, 6
California

The Zoo

Peacocks peep
Lions lurk
Tigers yap
Monkeys hang and jump.
And when the night moon comes out
And the stars glow brightly
All the animals cuddle up
And say goodnight.

Ogres

Ogres stomp
Ogres march
Ogres punch
Ogres growl.
And the best of all
When it's getting dark
They crawl into their caverns
And go to sleep.
And they stop stomping and marching and punching and growling.
Ogres dream about their next day.

Three Dragon Fish (Pen and acrylic marker)
Paris Andreou Hadjipavlou, 9
Cyprus

Alkkagi

A girl learns strategies for life by playing a traditional Korean game with her grandfather.

By Haeun Kim, 12
South Korea

In traditional Korea, there is a game that requires both sharp wit and quick, nimble fingers. Called *alkkagi* and translated literally as "shooting eggs," it is a game that is generally played by the older generation and enjoyed by the elderly, along with a glass of beer to wash the euphoria down. The gist of it is:

- A checkerboard
- Black and white "eggs"
- Sharp, strong fingers
- A voice to holler with

The goal of this game is to knock the other players' eggs out by flicking your eggs into the other players', forcing them to skid off the checkerboard and become "eliminated." The most slight miscalculations or awry positions can end a game; in the same way, a minuscule change of style can win it. To explain it broadly, it's "a game of simultaneously keeping away and drawing to each other," as my grandfather put it.

"You can't win by running away." His eyes smiled gently at me, glasses nestled on a hawkish nose. "But you can't win by running forward, either."

I straightened, my stubby legs curving with childish fat as I tucked them beneath me, the cushion shoved under my knees rubbing scratchily as I did so. "So, how do you win?" I demanded, glittering eyes fixed on the checkerboard. "How?"

His lips were pale, and his teeth shaded beneath them. His face looked sketched-in and wavering. "You wait," he said, his nose curving as he smiled, "and endure, and you take your chances as you get them." He scooped the eggs from the board and separated them into a black pile and a white pile. "Because the goal is not to win as fast as you can," he explained in his quivering, confused English. "It is just to have at least one chance left."

"Dad!" my mother complained, the left corner of her mouth curling up as she entered the dim, wooden room, "not now! Don't lecture her, she's just a little kid. She doesn't need to hear all your lessons."

She piled the papers into a stack and pushed them against the desk, slipping pens and pencils into a wooden drawer. Her eyes laughed brightly, devoid of unhappiness except for a lingering trace on her left palm, the tiny little crescent mark of fingernails biting angrily into her skin.

"When else will she hear this? When she has already forsaken it?" he asked, plucking one black egg from the white pile and moving it to the black pile. "She will never listen to this except for when her ears are still open. Imagine if they are closed! My words will pound against them and only close them further. Now is the only time when my words can enter unattacked."

My mother shook her head with her mouth pressed and ironed into a smile, her arms curling around to grab for my hand and reaching for my hair, stroking the bouncy curl that stuck up on my head. Her hand engulfed mine as she herded me away, her voice whisking back to my grandfather, "Be ready for dinner at seven!"

I reluctantly left, whipping my head back, my pigtails bouncing and battering the air, to see my grandfather's humbling smile. He had some secret that allowed him sure victory; I had no idea what it was, but I never won, and he never lost.

And so I grew up under the gentle governance of wisdom from my grandfather, the bright and colorful play of my grandmother, the complete and total, overwhelming love pouring from my mother, and the insistent kindness of my father. I grew without complaint and did so well; I was never reprimanded, and in turn, I refused to be.

I loved the game of alkkagi even when it became obsolete; I stayed in the dining room and watched, fascinated, as my parents shrieked and hollered delightedly, roaring with fury and jumping up with glee. I'd join in too, feeling the human desire to be involved, included, and do whatever it took not to be outside the circle. I'd scream with delight, mock my father as he groaned, insist on having a few more eggs, and take all my opportunities.

Then I grew to secondary school, and I changed my tactics—from that of a bumbling primary schooler who resorted to flicking eggs this way and that and only killing oneself—to keeping away. *Running away*, as my grandfather put it. I kept to the fringes and hoped that my defense could be my attack as well, and I rejected my chances as they laid themselves out on the board.

I suppose I hoped that someone would be reckless, taking chances not meant to be taken, and fall on their own swords, flicking their eggs the wrong way and losing while attempting to win. And that was well and all, but when I met with someone strategic and talented and someone who could hit me out, I stood no chance. I stood at the edges, hoping they'd knock themselves out along the way, only to be disappointed.

So neither way was the path to success. So then, what was it?

Practice, perhaps. And the right opportunities. Seizing the moment, as my father would say. And so I practiced—at what, I don't particularly know. I tried making the right decisions, choosing which battles to fight and which to accept. I sharpened my mind and sat down every week for a match of alkkagi with my parents.

My grandfather would say I practiced at life.

And then came a day when I didn't feel ready at all, when my bones were tired and my muscles felt stiff and my eyes were dry and aching; my eyelids were sandpaper. My mouth tasted parched, like sand and desert lingering in the air, that awful feeling of having woken up after sleeping with the mouth open and breathing. That, incidentally, was the day my grandfather decided to pay a visit, his alkkagi board in one hand and a wooden chest with both eggs mixed up in another.

"My girl," he said, his form shining like a mirage. Wavering, as if I was a starving, thirsty wanderer lost in the desert and dreaming of survival, of life, so desperately that I dreamed his existence. "Have you learned?" he asked. "Are you ready?"

I shook my head. "No," I said.

He nodded. "I was worried that you were." Quietly, as if telling a secret, he said, "Nothing ever happens when you're ready." He slipped past me and shut the door softly behind him, gesturing to the dining room and setting down the board, leaving me blinking and watching from the door.

"If one day you are to win at life," he asked, "don't you have to force certain days to be 'that day'? Won't you have to triumph over other strugglers? I have lived my life the way I have wanted to; my regrets are heavy, but they are not burdens. Now it is time for my descent, my downward spiral. My torch must be held by you. I am not ready for your triumph, but I have done all I can to ready you for it."

I laughed awkwardly, walking towards the dining room and flicking the lights on. "Grandpa, you make it sound like a huge battle or something," I teased, sitting down and casting my eyes about for my mother.

My grandfather watched impassively from the other side of the table. "You wanted to win. Do you still want this?"

I smiled. "Of course I do," I said. "But later, maybe, when I'm done with my homework. I have a lot of tests this week, see, and—"

"There will always be mountains, and you must always climb them. Do hikers never rest because there is still a mountain to climb?" My grandfather's voice was sharp and insistent, and I wanted to use my hollering voice to shout that he was wrong and old and decrepit and I knew better than he, but I pursed my lips and nodded instead.

"So why have you come?" I asked as I unfolded the checkerboard. "Did Grandma send you?"

My grandfather smiled, the first hint of emotion during this visit. "Yes, she did. She sent a bag of *goguma*. Sweet potato." He lifted a white-blue plastic bag from under the table, and I inhaled the flavor of the goguma through my nose, holding it there and savoring it.

"Thank you," I said, setting my pieces on the table. "Mom will love it."

"Of course she will. That is why your grandmother sent them. But let us delay no further. We must start eventually, and I will make that inevitable start to be now."

Ten minutes does not take particularly long, a blink of an eye to time, which has seen so much that is not interested in alkkagi matches between a girl and her masterful grandfather. But to the girl, it is everything. It is the moment she has waited for, what she has practiced for. This moment where she emerges victorious, where she triumphs over the past generation, proves herself worthy.

A little boy sits on the floor, moving around a toy car silently. His eyes flicker towards a huddle of shrieking, laughing boys playing soccer, and he casts his eyes downward desolately. He picks up his toy and moves towards them, but seems to think better of it and snaps the other way. His eyes are confused; he does not understand when this divide cracked between him and them.

His face is sour, cinched. It resembles a citrus fruit.

A woman with long hair and dark eyes reaches a hand towards the boy. "My boy," she says, "do you want to play soccer with them?"

"Not really." The boy swallows, and his eyes flicker again. "Not really."

There's a knowing look in the woman's eyes; a mother knows all. "Let me tell you a secret," she whispers, her arms curling around the boy and her chin resting on his shoulder. "In order to win—win life, or anything else of the sort, but life most of all—don't run away. You'll never win by running away. But then again," her eyes are yearning, nostalgic, "you'll never win by running forward, either."

The boy kicks out his feet and lashes his arms. "Then how?" he demands. "How do you win?"

"You wait," she says, her nose curving as she smiles, "and endure, and you take your chances as you get them."

She smiles as she remembers a hawkish nose, nestled glasses, a humbling smile; her grandfather, hunched over the checkerboard patiently—kind, patient eyes, a sketched face.

She smiles as she draws her son all the closer to her.

Generations fall, and new ones rise. Each is unique and flavorful and diverse, and each has a different strategy. Some hope famines and plagues will pass them by, others leap at wars and tumble with riots, and others wait and endure and take their chances as they get them.

égalitariste (Watercolor)
Verona Hofer, 12
California

Once

By Sascha Deal-Lessin, 12
New York

Once I saw the stars
Saw them in the dead of night
Once I saw the stars
Red and blue, dim and bright
Once I saw the stars
Twinkling in the sky
Once I saw the stars
Pure beauty to my eye
Once I saw the stars
But now the sky is gray and mean
And only planes are to be seen
But once I saw the stars.

Once I saw the fish
Saw them in the ocean blue
Once I saw the fish
Their scales held every hue
Once I saw the fish
Darting through the reef of coral
Once I saw the fish
Free of all the world's morals
Once I saw the fish
But now the water's green and stings
The ocean void of colorful things
But once I saw the fish

Once I saw the trees
Saw them in a city green
Once I saw the trees
Their leaves, a beautiful sheen
Once I saw the trees

Towering to the sky
Once I saw the trees
Though you may think that a lie
Once I saw the trees
But now the ground is bare and flat
No life round here except for rats
But once I saw the trees

Once I saw the art
Saw it in a building old
Once I saw the art
Too beautiful to be sold
Once I saw the art
Its vision made me think
Once I saw the art
So many shades of pink
Once I saw the art
But now the easels are cracked and torn
The fashion never to be worn
But once I saw the art

Once the world had beauty
And the stars all twinkled bright
Once the world had beauty
And the ocean was a sight
Once the world had beauty
With trees, lush and green
Once the world had beauty
With art that should be seen
Yes once the world had beauty
Where did it go?

Fallen (Acrylic)
Saira Merchant, 13
Texas

Glance (Graphite)

A stone's secret eyes

By Hazel Grace, 13
Massachusetts

A stone skips through the world,
Though unseen by the common eye.
Perhaps it begins out on the road, watching the mailman with his load.
As frost comes and all grows cold,
It rolls a way, by playfully running children's feet.
And now it's only half the size—
Has the world a plot for a stone so bold?
And then it's caught in someone's boot, taken far under foot.
It listens for a bit, to shouts of children making shaky self-portraits.
It's shaken loose by mother's hands and slips behind a drape's fold.
But that little stone a child spies: "A stone! A skipping stone!" she cries.
And off they run, to water's edge, and fling the stone, now just a pebble, high past
   the boat,
Like a water skimmer, it skips once, twice, thrice, four, five times…

Reflection

By Rou Rou Sem, 8
Washington

I see myself in it.
Everything looks the same.
My dark-as-night hair,
brown as a grizzly bear's eyes,
curvy ears,
hairy brows,
and pink nails.
It looks as if it was a duplicate of me.
When I move, it moves too.
When I look sad, it looks sad too.
When I look happy, it looks happy too.
But always when my mind drifts,
it always reminds me of me.

Reflection on Architecture (Canon Rebel)
Madeline Male, 14
Kansas

Imogen's Journey

After the terrors of *Kristallnacht*, Imogen's Jewish family must flee German-occupied Vienna.

By Camille Scott, 12
Texas

That morning, the Bernsteins had risen early, creating quite a commotion as they set about preparing breakfast and making sure nothing was going to be left behind. From the wailing of little Edna when she couldn't find her stuffed bear to the clatter of silverware in the sink and the hurry to get out the door, there had been no room to think—not then and not in the past week either.

Standing on the platform and waiting for her train, however, Imogen couldn't help but think back to what started it all, and why she was standing there that crisp morning, turning her back on Vienna.

9th of November—Kristallnacht

"Stop squirming, Edna," Imogen chided her younger sister.

"Hans! I want Hans!"

"Hans will be back soon. Stop acting like a two-year-old and start behaving like the four-year-old girl you are."

Edna practically worshiped her older brother—if anyone could get her to stop crying, he could, so Imogen was looking forward to his arrival home too.

"Where is Hans?"

"I told you. He is just down the street with *Mutti*. *Vater* will be back from work soon. What do you think of that? The whole family will be home. Now dry your eyes. This is no way to behave. What would your friends think if they saw you now?"

These words had a powerful effect. Edna wiped her snotty face and stopped crying immediately. She did so in perfect time—just after, the girls heard the door slam at the front of the apartment. "Is anyone home?"

Their father was back from his grocer's shop! Edna ran to the front of the home, squealing; Imogen followed at a more steady pace.

"Mutti and Hans are out at the butcher's. How was work?"

"Fine, fine. An ordinary day."

There was no question what this was, or who these people were trying to scare.

Forty-five minutes later, her mother and brother were still not back. Herr Bernstein grew worried, and questioned Imogen as to whether she was sure they had not planned to go anywhere else. As he scratched his head, Edna started to cry yet again for her older brother.

After an hour, there was a faint—and then louder—noise and shouting down below. Running to the living room window, they could see men with and without uniforms smashing and looting the shops in the street below, every one of which was Jewish-owned. The men harassed people in the street who were hurrying to get to the supposed safety of their homes. Even more frightening was the steady crackling and orange hue on the horizon—the local synagogue was burning.

There was no question what this was, or who these people were trying to scare.

"Papa," Imogen whispered. "What about Hans? And Mutti? They are not back yet."

A noise came from the stairwell. The party froze but breathed again when they heard a key in the lock—it was only Frau Bernstein.

"I am back. Don't you worry." Imogen's mother had come in breathlessly. "But Hans! He disappeared. I don't know what happened to him." Frau Bernstein had tears in her eyes. "He disappeared before it started . . . I don't know where he went, or if he thought it was some kind of joke, disappearing on me."

Again, there was a noise on the landing. However, this time instead of the reassuring noise of a key turning, someone knocked on the door.

"It could still be Hans!" Frau Bernstein cried, but Herr Bernstein stopped her. "But what if it's not?"

"Open up here or we'll force our way in!"—pounding on the door.

Despite her heart feeling as if it was in her throat, Imogen picked Edna up and ran to her bedroom at the back of the home. Their mother and father, meanwhile, surrendered and opened the door.

"Stay right there. Do not move." The voice was muffled from being all the way across the apartment but nevertheless loud and commanding. Imogen felt a shiver run down her spine.

Flushed and breathless, Imogen and her sister huddled behind the bed, Imogen keeping wiggling Edna in place.

The little girl opened her mouth to speak. "Be quiet, Edna!" It was said in a whisper, but Imogen still worried at the noise.

"Do not move while we search the house."

Footsteps moving towards the girls. A man at the door, briefly framed by the light in the hall before he stepped into the room with a short bark of something like laughter. "What sort of hiding place is that?"

Imogen and Edna were pushed towards the kitchen and made to stand up straight next to their parents.

Edna was trembling and crying as the two soldiers shoved her around. Hans was still not back. Imogen hung on to her one weapon: *Do not move. Stare straight ahead. Do not let them bother you. Do not let them see how you are feeling.*

In the end, Herr Bernstein managed to get himself released from the threat of deportation. However, it came at a cost—he and his family must be out of Austria by the following week.

Hans was gone—they heard from the butcher that he had been deported. This was a crushing revelation, but without any means to get him released, they had even worse things to worry about.

Like the fact that they had no visas.

Herr Bernstein had promised the soldier that they would get out, but the family had nowhere to go.

By the 15th of November, just two days before they had to be out of Austria, arrangements had been made.

Herr and Frau Bernstein, along with little Edna, were going to Poland. In Poland, Imogen's aunt lived with her husband and sons in Pastavy. There, they would be with close family.

Imogen, on the other hand, was to be sent to Switzerland. In Switzerland there was a good school where she could board. "The school has been very kind, taking you in on such short notice. You must work hard to repay their generosity, get your education, and study. One day all of this will be over." Nobody could say when. "Edna . . . she is too little. Edna needs her parents."

I need my parents, was Imogen's thought as she stood on that platform, her parents having left only a few minutes previously on a train to Warsaw, from where they would travel to Pastavy. However, Imogen knew that she was plenty old enough to go on the journey—she was just plain *scared*.

Shutting her eyes tight, Imogen blocked out the station entirely. *Think of a good time before the occupation.*

Slowly, it came, then all in a rush: School, laughing with her friends. The block that her apartment looked over, quiet and serene but for the laughing and shouting of the local children playing. Sailing somewhere she couldn't quite remember . . . possibly somewhere else in Austria. Her bat mitzvah, a year and a half ago now.

That was where the memories stopped, though. Instead, she found herself looking into the future. What would she find in Switzerland? Imogen did not have the faintest idea. She would have a place to sleep, a place to learn, a place that would offer refuge from the danger of Vienna . . . but would she find a home?

Imogen no longer had a home in the place that she grew up. The soldiers had turned her beautiful hometown into a place she did not recognize, a place where she was not welcome.

Would she ever regain her home—or find another one? What did the years ahead hold?

Sunflower Shades (Pen and pastel)
Riya Kasture, 12
India

Imogen was conveniently bumped and chastised—"You! Watch out, there!"—just in time for the conductor to yell, "Last call, route to Zurich!"

Imogen needed to get onto the train. Fast.

Through the crowd, jumping on at the last minute . . . the toot of the horn, and the doors closed. The train was moving, and the station was left long behind by the time Imogen found her seat.

Stop being so sentimental, she told herself. *Stop thinking about things when you can't change them, when they'll only make you sadder. Maybe it's better you didn't get to look at Vienna one last time. Besides, you'll see Mutter and Vater again soon.*

After a moment, *You'll even see Hans.*

Hans . . . what was Hans doing at this moment? Was he even still alive? The idea that the answer to that latter question might be no scared her, but it was undeniably true.

Imogen was surprised to find a single tear on her cheek. She never cried. Not once the past year had she shed a tear, not when Germany invaded and anti-Semitism had grown too close to her little neighborhood in Vienna, not even when Kristallnacht had arrived and Hans was taken away. Yet she was crying now, crying for Hans and Edna and her mother and father and every one of her neighbors who was in danger.

But Imogen realized something, and what she realized was also scary, yet somehow comforting as well: *I can't change it either way, and there is no way of knowing. If I think Hans might not be alive, I will only make myself more miserable with the uncertainty.*

Instead, have hope.

As the train settled into its rhythm, and yellow grass and green bushes flew past, although the girl still found herself shedding a tear or two, one thing kept her going, over and over:

Better to have hope.

Scan this QR code to access educational material for this painting.

Face (Oil)
Crystal Fu, 12
New York

Random Volcano (Acrylic)
Patrick Nguyen, 7
Wisconsin

Feelings

By Teagen Christensen, 12
Washington

My
best friend
devoured
my heart
My Vision
was changed. I
dragged
myself forward.
I see someone
disappear
in the
distance.
I think
I am
not myself

Into the Unknown (Samsung Galaxy S21)
Bala Harini Ramesh, 11
North Carolina

Just Imagine

By Mirabel Sandler, 7
California

Trees instead of poles
Mountains instead of buildings
Rivers instead of roads
Boulders instead of cars

Flowers instead of litter
Grass instead of stores
Forests instead of parking lots
Sunsets instead of smog

Oceans instead of cities
Lakes instead of concrete
Dolphins instead of ships
Meadows instead of machines

Mechanical things devour the earth like a fox hunts a rabbit,
making their own islands
while crumpling the world to pieces.

The moon stares down upon us with love.
The trees give us their shade with kindness
while all we see is an ax.

The earth is not a huge clump of metal.
We must see it in a different way,
like the beauty it is.

That's the world we should be.
That's the world we should see.

Frog Life (Galaxy A32)
Emma Catherine Hoff, 11
New York

Indiana Wind Farm

By Ian Maduff, 11
Illinois

Through the afternoon
In a blue Honda Fit
In toward the wind farm
We shall go.

As the wind turbines spin
In the afternoon wind
Shadows on the ground
Like a fidget.

In the high winds
You feel like you can touch it
But cannot
Car shadows go.

Spinning shadows
Of the turbines
Night and Day
Out in the plains.

Glow of the farm
Of the sunlight
Beating down
The wind farm spins.

Through the wind farm
We shall go
The sun goes down
Driving toward Illinois.

Spinning turbines
In high winds
The shadow spins
On the highway.

Spinning very fast
Fast as you go
The wind shall blow
Is how the turbine goes.

Two Poems

By Emma Catherine Hoff, 11
New York

Explosion in a Shingle Factory

The stairs collapsed beneath her
and as she fell, she prayed for her body
not to be seen, not painted by a brush,
she saw the sun, then the moon,
nighttime descended as splinters of wood
flew into her eyes, poured out of her mouth,
sinking past an assortment of floating objects—
a banjo is her head, her torso is a Picasso painting,
her legs are brooms, sweeping the air, her arms
are cut-up cloth.

Curious eyes peek over the crumbling banister,
which a disembodied yet still whole hand holds on to,
but soon the skin peels away, leaving only bone,
which also disappears—everything is still and dark,
alone and quiet, somewhere the nude is still falling.

Automat by Edward Hopper

It doesn't look like an automat,
just a building that reeks of steel
and machinery and aching backs,
with a corner in which a woman sits
at a table, invisible to everyone,
scowling into her cup of tea.

She had given up on pounding on doors
long ago, knowing that nobody would let
her in; she depended on her green jacket
for comfort, occasionally peeking down,
past the yellow banister, to the dark room
from which she heard laughter.

They did the best they could, said one
brown lock of hair that curved around her
shoulder, tickling her neck—but the other
said in her ear, *Go downstairs, and
throw your fruit at the ungrateful
people in the basement.*

The bowl of fruit appeared, but she kept
still and made no comment—she heard nothing,
only the sound of the rain outside,
and the teacup against the blue table,
and the moths banging against the flickering
yellow lights.

The laughing people came upstairs
and stopped in front of her table.
Still chuckling, they said,
Give us a smile! Give us a smile!

Golden Muse and Sun Flowers (Acrylic)
Arwen Gamez, 14
New York

An Unusual Haircut

Carys and her family shave their heads in support of her grandmother, who has cancer.

By Carys Kim, 9
California

Bzzzzzzzzzzz. The clipper buzzed through my brother Noah's hair. It was a blazing hot summer day, and I was at my grandma's house. We were outside on the patio. I shook my legs and tapped my toes nervously on the creaky wooden floor. My grandma had lung cancer, and her hair was falling out. She had been sick for a long time, but recently, we had all decided that our whole family would shave our heads. It was a rare thing for girls to do, so it was a hard decision for my mom and me. Just a few days ago, my mom and I agreed that we would do it too. I watched sadly as my brother's hair slowly fell to the floor. My fluffy, cute dog, Bingsoo, sniffed the hair and scurried around.

"You're done, Noah. You can come now, Carys," my dad said calmly, wiping his forehead with his shirt. Noah hopped off the chair and went to go to the shower. My heart beat loudly. I had so many questions. What would I look like? Would other people like it? Would I like it? I had easily agreed before, but now, looking at all the sharp tools my dad had and realizing how hard it would actually be, I felt scared. There were butterflies flying around in my stomach, and I felt worried.

I gulped and took a wobbly step onto the wooden floor. I stepped over piles of hair and took a deep breath. My legs felt like Jell-O, and my hands were clenched and sweaty. My heart pounded in my chest, and my teeth were gritted. I slowly advanced across the floor and carefully sat on the chair, my heart beating fast and loud. I was dripping with sweat. From the heat—but mostly because of my nervousness. My mom took a picture of me, and I tried my best to smile.

"You ready, Carys?" my dad asked. I took a shaky breath. Bingsoo whined and pawed at the seat. I gave her a little scratch behind the ear. *I need to do this,* I thought. I looked at my grandma. *Okay. I CAN do this,* I thought, clenching my sweaty hands. My throat felt dry, and so did my lips.

"O-okay," I said bravely. I heard a click, and I expected to hear buzzing, but then suddenly . . .

Snap!

"Aaaah!!" I exclaimed, surprised. "My braids!" I said, feeling the top of my hair. Yup. They were gone! My dad handed me my braids. My family was all smiling. Why were they smiling? They were so calm, while I was having the scariest moment of my life! My heart beat fast. My mom brought a mirror for me to see myself. I was almost too scared to look at it. My hand trembled, and my toes twitched. I grabbed the mirror's handle weakly, and I held it facedown. I looked at my mom and dad. They both looked happy. I felt reassured, and I turned the mirror around, ready to see how horrible I would look. I held it up to my face, and my eyes went wide. I looked . . . I actually looked . . . funny! I started laughing, and my mom snapped another picture. My dad continued buzzing my hair off. *Bzzzzzzzzzzzzz.* The clipper buzzed and buzzed and buzzed. It sounded like one million bees buzzing at the same time. The smell of sweat filled the patio.

I looked at the calm reflection of the swimming pool water. It looked peaceful. I focused my vision on the small waves in the water. *Bzzzzzzzzzzzzzzz.* Hair fell to the floor and piled up on my shoulders and my shirt. I felt the itchiness of the hair on me. I shifted in the chair, trying to shake some of the itchy hair off.

"Stay still, Carys," my dad warned. I kept as still as I could. *Bzzzzzzzzzzzzz. Bzzzzzzzzzzzzzzzz. Bzzzzzzzzzzzzzzzzzz.* The buzzing sound broke through the air. My stomach grumbled. Bingsoo sniffed more hair and occasionally took a nibble. The sky was pale blue and with streaks of white clouds. It was late afternoon and the sun was shining in the sky. I fiddled with my fingers and made shapes with the clouds. Oh, that one's a rabbit. *Now a bird . . .* I thought. I zoned off for what seemed like forever until, "Carys! You're done!" my dad exclaimed. I looked up and saw myself in the mirror.

"Wow! I look . . ." I felt my head. It felt spiky, yet furry. My body was trembling, and my heart swelled with pride. I did it. I had actually done it. I had done this all for my grandma. The buzzing sound echoed in my head. I remembered the time . . . which was only a few hours ago, my nervousness and when my braids . . . *snap!* Right off my head. This was a day I will never, ever, forget in my entire life. I felt a new kind of strength, for my grandma, my family, and most of all . . . myself.

Evening Swing (iPhone 8)
Tatum Lovely, 12
Pennsylvania

Within the Stars

After the death of her husband, Olive discovers the healing power of creativity.

By Mia Atkinson, 11
California

Olive didn't know how long she'd sat on her bed staring at the stars. They were so bright that night, shining like thousands of little suns in the sky. It brightened up the window next to her bed, its paper-white curtain fully open.

Olive sighed, a sound like a balloon deflating. She felt like that. Ten years ago, Olive had sat on this very bed, holding her breath and silently praying to the stars as her husband took his last breaths from a fever. They were too poor to pay for a doctor to come to their house, and going there would just take too long.

That was when she lost her husband.

That was when she became no one.

That was when she became just an old woman with frail hands.

Just.

Olive wiped away a tear, staring at the full sky. The wind through the open window tickled her cheek as she stared out at the stars. She imagined that they were reaching out to her, glowing brightly. Her husband was up there too, waving at her and telling her that she would be all right, even though they both knew she wouldn't. Not without him . . .

Olive only looked down when she felt something brush against her leg. Gasping with surprise, she found her old embroidery kit, unfinished, with unraveling thread. Olive blinked, then picked up her kit, staring at the unfinished picture she had started. Her eyes welled with tears.

"It's the sky," Olive murmured, almost more to the embroidery than to herself. "The night sky." Memories flashed behind Olive's head: Her husband asking her to do one of the night skies. Her agreeing. Her getting started. And now, her not finishing, not having time to finish. Embroidery was one of her husband's favorite things to do. It would certainly be nice if Olive finished this piece for him. But she couldn't . . . ever since his death, she couldn't . . .

"It'll be good." Olive hadn't realized that the words had come from her until moments later. "It'll be good." She said the words again, trying to convince herself that it was the right choice. "It'll help me."

The last words were the ones that sealed the box and sent it away. Olive would do it. *It'll help me.*

So Olive got to work, stitching her way through the embroidery, just like she used to. Her hands were more shaky and weak than she had remembered, but overall she was confident. Olive repeated the words inside her mind: back stitch, chain stitch, French knot, running stitch. She knew exactly what to do and how to do it. Staring at the stars for days and days on end had finally paid off.

As Olive continued to stitch, she felt her insides loosen up, and all her worries and terrible thoughts began to float away from her. This feeling was what she really missed, to feel so free and creative and open. And when Olive looked down at her work an hour later, she realized that she had finished all but a little triangle of space in the right corner. She just needed to complete the final piece. Olive was finishing her embroidery and healing her broken insides with that last stitch.

She knew what to do.

Through the Hand Lens (iPhone SE)
Madeline Cleveland, 13
Wisconsin

Just One

By Charlotte Rosenthal-Noble, 8
Vermont

You are just one
apple on a whole
apple tree
but the smallest seed
will make the biggest difference
eventually

Highlight from Stonesoup.com

The First Snow
By Evelyn Lien

Linda sat on the porch watching the clouds, and occasionally, the butterflies fluttering over the front yard. Ever since she'd been diagnosed with late-stage breast cancer last year, she started to slow down and to appreciate the simple yet beautiful things all around her so much more.

Suddenly, she heard loud footsteps.

It must be Charlotte, Linda thought.

Sure enough, her five-year-old daughter, Charlotte, came running around to the porch and sat down next to her.

Linda noticed Charlotte's unusual air of sadness.

"What's up, sweetie?" Linda asked.

Charlotte turned and gave her a smile. "Mommy, I miss our old house."

"You don't like this new house?" Linda asked.

"I like it, but Daddy said it doesn't really snow in Texas, even in winter. I miss the snow. It would always look like magic!" Charlotte said. She loved playing on snow days with her friends.

Linda and her family used to live in Illinois, where it snowed a lot in the winter. But they recently moved south to Texas because it's closer to Linda's parents who can help take care of Charlotte.

She saw disappointment briefly flash over Charlotte's face.

"You know what? Actually, it does snow in Texas sometimes. Just not that much, though!" Linda said, in an attempt to cheer Charlotte up.

"Really?!" Charlotte's face brightened up. "I wish I could see the snow . . . with you!"

"Of course, sweetie! When the next snow comes, you and I will be together." Linda pointed at the front lawn and said, "Right over there, watching the beautiful white magic falling down."

You can read the rest of Evelyn's story at https://stonesoup.com/post/stone-soup-monthly-flash-contest-winners-roll/

About the Flash Contests

Stone Soup holds a flash contest during the first week of every month. The month's first Weekly Creativity prompt provides the contest challenge. Submissions are due by midnight on Sunday of the same week. Up to five winners are chosen for publication on our blog. The winners, along with up to five honorable mentions, are announced in the following Saturday newsletter. Find all the details at stonesoup.com/post/stone-soup-monthly-flash-contest-winners-roll/

Honor Roll

Welcome to the Stone Soup Honor Roll. Every month, we receive submissions from hundreds of kids from around the world. Unfortunately, we don't have space to publish all the great work we receive. We want to commend some of these talented writers and artists and encourage them to keep creating.

FICTION

Zea Arbuckle, 9
Dylan Ecimovic, 13
Victoria Gong, 11
Liam Hubbard, 11
Isabella Kim, 12
Zoe Li, 10
Gavin Liu, 13
Vivian Palme, 10
Olivia Puleo, 13
Yueling Qian, 11
Olivia Rhee, 13
Meg Schmitt, 10
Siaansh Singh Bhadauria, 12
Maya Walsh, 10
Parker White, 12
Ellie Wang, 10
Xi Zhao, 14
Anthony Zhang, 11

POETRY

Anaya Chougule, 12
Adalin DeMarco, 10
Rocco Russo, 11
Grace Scherer, 11
Ilina Singh, 13
Anushka Trivedi, 12
Kyra Welton, 13

MEMOIR

Camilla Henneberger, 11
Mina Stigsgaard, 11
Soyori Suzuki, 12

ART

Gio Hyung, 11
Amaya Cardoza Mo, 11
Sullivan Vega, 5

Visit the Stone Soup Store at Amazon.com/stonesoup

At our store, you will find . . .

- Current and back issues of *Stone Soup*

- Our growing collection of books by young authors, as well as themed anthologies

- Journals and sketchbooks

. . . and more!

Finally, don't forget to visit Stonesoup.com to browse our bonus materials. There you will find:

- Information about our writing workshops

- Monthly flash contests and weekly creativity prompts

- Blog posts from our young bloggers on everything from sports to sewing

- Video interviews with *Stone Soup* authors

. . . and more content by young creators!

Scan this to visit *Stone Soup* online!

Printed in the USA
CPSIA information can be obtained
at www.ICGtesting.com
CBHW050723081023
1260CB00001B/1

9 780894 091513